Dear Parent:

Congratulations! Your child is taking
the first steps on an exciting journey.
The destination? Independent reading!

STEP INTO READING® will help your child get there. The program offers
five steps to reading success. Each step includes fun stories and colorful art.
There are also Step into Reading Sticker Books, Step into Reading Math
Readers, Step into Reading Write-In Readers, Step into Reading Phonics
Readers, and Step into Reading Phonics First Steps! Boxed Sets—a complete
literacy program with something for every child.

Learning to Read, Step by Step!

Ready to Read Preschool–Kindergarten
• big type and easy words • rhyme and rhythm • picture clues
For children who know the alphabet and are eager to
begin reading.

Reading with Help Preschool–Grade 1
• basic vocabulary • short sentences • simple stories
For children who recognize familiar words and sound out
new words with help.

Reading on Your Own Grades 1–3
• engaging characters • easy-to-follow plots • popular topics
For children who are ready to read on their own.

Reading Paragraphs Grades 2–3
• challenging vocabulary • short paragraphs • exciting stories
For newly independent readers who read simple sentences
with confidence.

Ready for Chapters Grades 2–4
• chapters • longer paragraphs • full-color art
For children who want to take the plunge into chapter books
but still like colorful pictures.

STEP INTO READING® is designed to give every child a successful
reading experience. The grade levels are only guides. Children can progress
through the steps at their own speed, developing confidence in their
reading, no matter what their grade.

Remember, a lifetime love of reading starts with a single step!

www.stepintoreading.com

Educators and librarians, for a variety of teaching tools, visit us at
www.randomhouse.com/teachers

Library of Congress Cataloging-in-Publication Data
Little, Emily.
David and the giant / by Emily Little ; illustrated by Hans Wilhelm.
  p. cm. — (Step into reading. A step 2 book)
Originally published: New York : Random House, c1987.
SUMMARY: A simple retelling of the Old Testament story of the shepherd boy David, whose faith in God helped him overcome the Philistine giant Goliath.
ISBN 0-394-88867-7 (trade) — ISBN 0-394-98867-1 (lib. bdg.)
1. David, King of Israel—Juvenile literature. 2. Goliath (Biblical giant)—Juvenile literature. 3. Bible stories, English—O.T. Samuel, 1st. [1. David, King of Israel. 2. Goliath (Biblical giant). 3. Bible stories—O.T.]
I. Wilhelm, Hans, 1945– ill. II. Title. III. Series: Step into reading. Step 2 book.
BS580.D3 L55 2003 222'.4309505—dc21 2002015236

Printed in the United States of America 35

DAVID
AND THE
GIANT

By Emily Little

Illustrated by Hans Wilhelm

Random House New York

Long ago
there was a boy
named David.
David looked after
his father's sheep.
And God looked after David.

Once a lion came
to steal a sheep.
Was David afraid? No!

He killed the lion
all by himself!

Soon war came
to David's land.
David's brothers
went off to fight.

But David was too young.

He had to stay at home.

One day
David's father said,
"You must take some food
to your brothers."

So David did.
He walked
all the way
to the top of a hill.

David saw his brothers.

He saw the king.

He saw lots of other men, too.

But no one saw David.
Everyone was looking
at the other army.
When would the battle begin?

Then—
across the valley
came a giant.
The giant was big
and strong
and mean.

"I am Goliath.
Send one man
to fight me!"
shouted the giant.
"And if I kill him,
you will be our slaves."

The king asked,
"Who will fight Goliath?"
"Not me! Not me!"
cried the men.

Then David said,
"Send me.
I will fight
the giant."

David's brothers said,
"No! You are too small.
Goliath is so big!"

But the king said,

"Let David go."

The king gave David
a big sword.
David gave it back.
"I have my sling,"
he said.

Goliath laughed at David.
"Come!" he cried.
"Let me turn you
into food
for the birds!"
Was David afraid?
No!
"God will look after me,"
David said.

The giant laughed again.
He made fun
of David's God.
David picked up a stone.
He put it in his sling.

ZING!

The stone hit Goliath

between the eyes!

The giant
fell down—
dead!

"The boy killed Goliath!"
cried Goliath's men.
"Run for your lives!"

Goliath's army ran away.

The war was over.

David heard cheering.
His brothers lifted
him up.
Everyone was shouting
David's name.

David was a hero!

David grew up
to be a great king.
He looked after
all his people.

And God still
looked after David.